Twenty-Four ROBBERS

Audrey Wood

Child's Play (International) Ltd

Swindon   Auburn ME   Sydney

© 1980 M. Twinn   This edition 2004
ISBN 1-904550-35-5   Printed in Croatia

1 3 5 7 9 10 8 6 4 2
www.childs-play.com

Not last night, but the night before…

Twenty-four robbers came a-knocking at my door.

I asked them what they wanted,

And this is what they said...

"H-O-T...

...Hot Peppers !!!"

I gave them my peppers, and then they rode away.

But twenty-four robbers came back the next day.

I asked them what they wanted,

And this is what they said...

"H-O-T...

..Hot Peppers !!!"

I didn't have peppers, so they took a cob of corn,

And twenty-four robbers said, "See you in the morn!"

Just this morn, not the morn before,

Twenty-four robbers came a-knocking at my door.

I asked them what they wanted, and this is what they said...

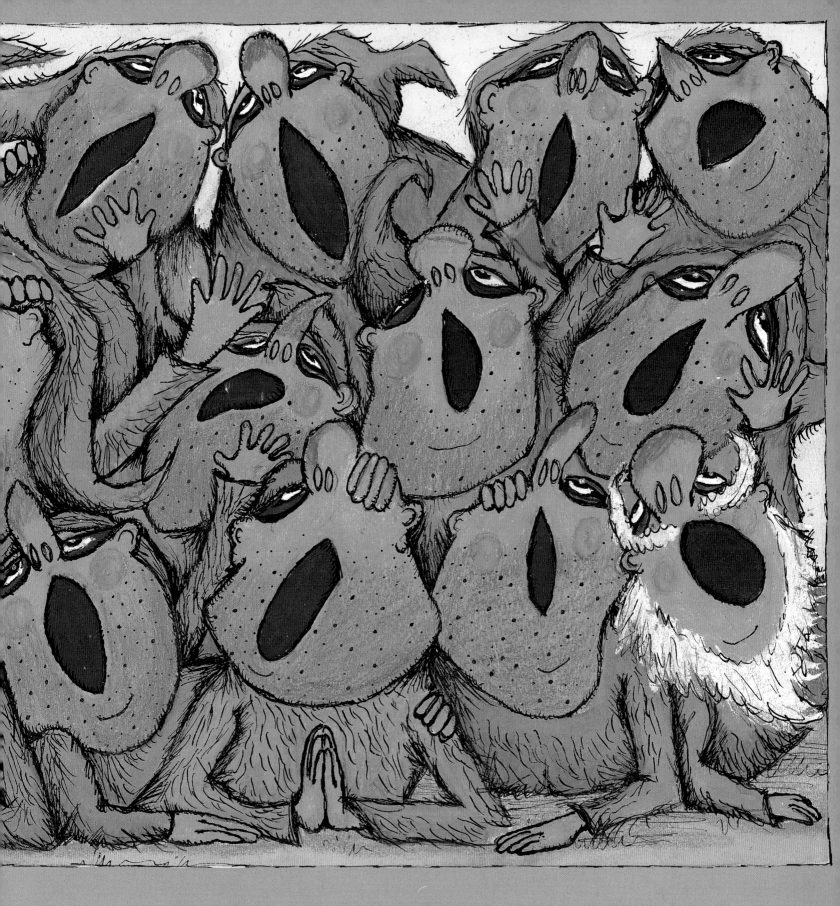

"C - O - R - N.....Corn !!!"

I didn't have corn, but I had a little flour.

They put it in their sack and said, "See you in an hour!"

Not this hour, but the hour before,

Twenty-four robbers came a-knocking at my door.

I opened my door. I saw they had a pot.

And twenty-four robbers said, "We like you a lot!"

"You gave us your peppers! You gave us your corn!

You gave us your flour, early in the morn!"

Now here is what they did, and this is all true.

They gave me a pot of hot pepper stew.

"H-O-T...

...Hot Peppers !!!"

The End